Pebble

Dogs

Jack Russell Terriers

by Jody Sullivan Rake

Consulting Editor: Gail Saunders-Smith, PhD

Consultant: Jennifer Zablotny, DVM
Member, American Veterinary Medical Association

Capstone
press

Mankato, Minnesota

Pebble Books are published by Capstone Press,
151 Good Counsel Drive, P.O. Box 669, Mankato, Minnesota 56002.
www.capstonepress.com

1 2 3 4 5 6 12 11 10 09 08 07

Library of Congress Cataloging-in-Publication Data
Rake, Jody Sullivan.
    Jack Russell terriers / by Jody Sullivan Rake.
    p. cm.—(Pebble Books. Dogs)
    Summary: "Summary: Simple text and photographs introduce the Jack Russell
terrier breed, its growth from puppy to adult, and pet care information"—Provided
by publisher.
    Includes bibliographical references and index.
    ISBN-13: 978-0-7368-6743-6 (hardcover)
    ISBN-10: 0-7368-6743-0 (hardcover)
    1. Jack Russell terrier—Juvenile literature. I. Title. II. Series.
SF429.J27R35 2007
636.755—dc22   2006028392

Note to Parents and Teachers

The Dogs set supports national science standards related to life science. This book describes and illustrates Jack Russell terriers. The images support early readers in understanding the text. The repetition of words and phrases helps early readers learn new words. This book also introduces early readers to subject-specific vocabulary words, which are defined in the Glossary section. Early readers may need assistance to read some words and to use the Table of Contents, Glossary, Read More, Internet Sites, and Index sections of the book.

Table of Contents

Daring Diggers

Jack Russell terriers love to dig in the dirt. They are also called Parson Russell terriers.

Jack Russell terriers
chase almost anything
that moves.
They run after gophers
and other small animals.

From Puppy to Adult

As many as eight terrier
puppies can be born
in one litter.
They stay with their mother
for about three months.

At three months,
the puppies are
curious and active.
They need training
to learn good behavior.

Jack Russell terriers
grow to be
about as tall as a ruler.
They are small, but they
have lots of energy.

Terrier Care

Jack Russell terriers should walk, run, and play at least once a day. At home, they need a safe yard with a fence.

Terriers need food
and clean water.
They need more
food and water when
they run and play a lot.

Terriers shed their hair all year long. Owners should brush their dogs once a week.

Lots of time and love
from their owners
make Jack Russell terriers
happy dogs.

Glossary

active—being busy and moving around a lot; Jack Russell terriers are very active dogs; they need lots of exercise and activity.

chase—to run after something; Jack Russell terriers often chase after gophers, foxes, and other small animals.

curious—eager to explore and learn about new things

litter—a group of young born to one mother at the same time

training—teaching an animal to do what you say

Read More

Murray, Julie. *Jack Russell Terriers.* Animal Kingdom. Edina, Minn.: Abdo, 2005.

Temple, Bob. *Jack Russell Terriers.* Checkerboard Animal Library. Edina, Minn.: Abdo, 2000.

Internet Sites

FactHound offers a safe, fun way to find Internet sites related to this book. All of the sites on FactHound have been researched by our staff.

Here's how:

1. Visit *www.facthound.com*
2. Choose your grade level.
3. Type in this book ID **0736867430** for age-appropriate sites. You may also browse subjects by clicking on letters, or by clicking on pictures and words.
4. Click on the **Fetch It** button.

FactHound will fetch the best sites for you!

23

Index

Word Count: 161
Grade: 1
Early-Intervention Level: 16

Editorial Credits
Mari Schuh, editor; Juliette Peters, set designer; Kyle Grenz, book designer;
  Kara Birr, photo researcher; Scott Thoms, photo editor

Photo Credits
Ardea/John Daniels, 12; Capstone Press/Karon Dubke, 16, 18, 20; Corbis/DLILLC,
6; Corbis/Royalty-Free, cover; Photo by Fiona Green, 4; Ron Kimball Stock/Renee
Stockdale, 8; Shutterstock/Jeffrey Ong Guo Xiong, 1; Shutterstock/Stephen Walls, 10;
Superstock/age fotostock, 14